Curtis the Crab

A Chesapeake Bay Adventure

By Cindy Freland

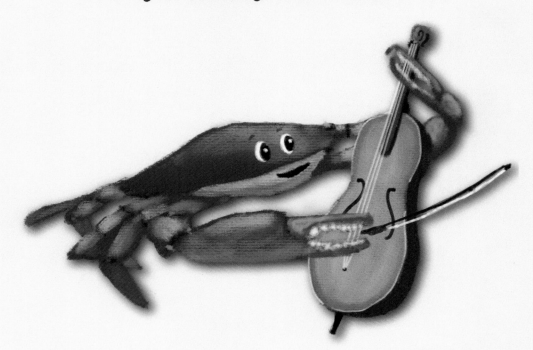

This book is dedicated to my beautiful daughters,

Andrea and Alyssa Bean

Thanks for all the encouragement, love and laughter. I love you!

NO SWIMMING! Jason was shocked to read the huge sign that said there was no swimming allowed at North Beach. But how could this be? "I just swam here last summer," he thought to himself.

The sign read:
"NO SWIMMING! All beaches around the Chesapeake Bay are polluted. The water is dangerous and the sand contains broken glass. Toxins in the water will make you sick."

"Oh, no! How could this be? I loved swimming in the bay and playing in the sand," thought Jason.

But the sign was right. The beach was covered in Styrofoam cups, paper plates, empty bottles, cigarette butts and other trash. The water was dirty and there were lots of dead fish in the sand.

"I wonder what "toxins" are in the water to make it so bad where we cannot swim," thought Jason.

Jason woke up from his dream. He was so glad it wasn't real. Even though he knew it was only a dream, he wanted to find out if it was true. Could there really be that many toxins in the water to make it dangerous where no one could swim? Where could he find out?

He asked his mom where he could find the answer but she didn't know. Jason asked his dad but he didn't know. He asked his teacher. She didn't know but she told him to go to the beach and ask the park ranger. The ranger would know the answer.

So the next day Jason asked his mom if she would take him to the beach. He just had to find out about the toxins in the water that

were in his dream. "Let's go on Saturday and spend the whole day there. We will bring a picnic lunch," she said.

Jason was so excited about going to Breezy Point Beach in Chesapeake Beach, Maryland. He loved body surfing and playing in the sand. He made huge sand castles and forts.

His mom packed their lunch in the blue and white cooler. They ate chicken salad sandwiches on rolls, potato chips and grapes with water to drink.

Then Jason went into the water to swim. He noticed a paper cup floating in the water. Then he saw more trash. He wondered if this was the "toxin" in his dream. Then he remembered the whole reason he went to the beach was to ask the park ranger about the water pollution.

Jason asked his mom if he could talk to the park ranger. She told him that he could. So off he went to find the ranger. The ranger was talking to a group of children about keeping the beach clean. She told Jason he could come in and have a seat.

The ranger said, "My name is Ranger Amy. I am in charge at Breezy Point Beach. My job is to keep the beach safe and clean. But when it is not clean, I need to find out why."

Jason raised his hand and asked, "Ranger Amy, why is trash in the water?"

"Trash in the water is one of the main reasons I am here to help you learn. It takes all of us to keep it clean, including you and your parents. If you leave a plastic bag or a drink can in the sand, the tide will wash it into the water. Birds and fish may eat the trash and it may hurt or kill them. Please ask your parents to help by

putting trash in the trash cans, or better yet, take it with you. We also need to check with the factories. There are chemicals going into the water," Ranger Amy said.

Now Jason knew a little more about the toxins in the water. He will tell his parents and friends what he learned so they could help too.

Now it's time for more fun. He wanted to go crabbing so he asked his mom if he could. They walked to the pier and saw a man and his children crabbing. The man and his children were laughing and having such a good time. They already had many crabs in the big, orange bucket. Jason walked up to the man and said, "May I please try it?"

The man gave Jason a chicken neck to tie on a string and said, "Just put the string into the water near the pier and maybe you will catch a crab."

Within just a few minutes Jason was yelling, "I CAUGHT A CRAB, I CAUGHT A CRAB." Jason's yelling scared Curtis the Crab so much that Curtis let go of the chicken neck and fell back into the water.

Curtis was so scared that he swam as fast as he could to get away. He forgot what he was supposed to do. He needed to find four musicians to play in the concert in two days.

The concert was to help attract more crabs and oysters to the Chesapeake Bay. The numbers were so low because of overfishing and pollution that Curtis decided to do something about it. He would find the musicians and ask them to play in the concert in

Crab Alley Bay. Traveling to Herring Bay, West River, Eastern Bay and then to Crab Alley Bay would take time and it would be dangerous.

It was a very hot day in September and the peak of crab season. That meant there were lots of big crabs in the water and lots of people trying to catch them. Curtis had to be careful if he wanted to find the musicians and make it to the concert.

Oakley the Oyster played the piano in Herring Bay. Bethany the Bass played the harp in West River. Sampson the Seahorse played the flute in Eastern Bay. Celia the Catfish played the violin in Crab Alley Bay. Curtis played the cello and he lived in Mayo Beach.

How could Curtis find all those musicians in only two days? He better be on his way. First he had to find Oakley the Oyster in Herring Bay and ask him to play the piano. He had an idea that

was very dangerous but it would help him get to Herring Bay much quicker.

Curtis remembered how easy it was getting caught by the boy. All he needed to do was find a pier and look for humans that were crabbing. He looked around and found two boys with strings and a net. So Curtis positioned himself on the post near the pier in hopes one of the boys would drop a string.

Sure enough! Within just a few minutes Curtis was going for the chicken neck attached to the string. One of the boys yelled, "I CAUGHT A CRAB! I CAUGHT A CRAB!" The other boy grabbed the net and scooped up Curtis to put him in the orange bucket.

But Olivia the Osprey was hunting for fish to feed her family. She spotted her friend, Curtis, on the string and swooped down to help him. Before the boy could get Curtis into the bucket, Olivia

grabbed Curtis with her sharp talons and carried him off to her nest.

Curtis was not happy. He said, "Olivia, thanks so much for rescuing me, but I am TRYING to get caught."

"TRYING to get caught?" asked Olivia.

"Yes, I need a fast way to get to Herring Bay. I want to talk to Oakley the Oyster. We are having a concert in two days and I don't have much time. I need to get a ride on a truck filled with crabs," said Curtis.

"Why didn't you ask me to help? You don't have to get caught to get into the truck. I can carry you there and drop you," said Olivia.

So Olivia gently picked up Curtis in her talons and flew away with him. Together they searched for a truck filled with baskets of crabs.

"I SEE ONE!" yelled Olivia. Olivia flew closer and closer until she got almost to the truck. She gently dropped Curtis. He landed on the hard bed of an old, red farm truck. But Curtis was okay and Olivia flew back to her nest to check on her family.

Curtis was scared as he had never been on a truck. He saw the crabs moving and he could hear them scratching the baskets. Curtis asked one of the crabs if they were going to Herring Bay. "Yes, we are going to a party there," said Calleigh the Crab. She was very excited.

"Do you know Oakley the Oyster?" Curtis asked Calleigh.

"Yes, he lives near the pier on the sunny side of the restaurant," Calleigh said.

"We are going to have a concert to attract more crabs and oysters to the bay. Please tell everyone. Thanks for your help," said Curtis.

When the truck finally stopped, men jumped out and slammed the truck doors. More men came running out of the restaurant. During all the commotion, Curtis jumped off the truck. Now he had to get into the water very quickly or he would dry up.

Curtis found a puddle that was melted ice and stayed there for a few minutes. He could feel the sun beating down on his blue shell. Men were running all around so he needed to get back into the bay. He ran very quickly and jumped into the water.

Now that Curtis was finally in Herring Bay, he needed to find Oakley the Oyster quickly. He swam over to the sunny side of the restaurant and found him in the mud on the bottom of the bay.

"Oakley, would you like to play the piano in a concert in two days? It's to help attract more crabs and oysters to the bay," said Curtis.

"I would love to help," said Oakley.

"I need to find Bethany the Bass in West River to play the harp, Sampson the Seahorse in Eastern Bay to play the flute and Celia the Catfish in Crab Alley Bay to play the violin. Will you please help me find them?" said Curtis.

"Sure, I will help you," said Oakley.

"Thanks for your help," said Curtis.

In the meantime, Calleigh the Crab started telling other crabs about the concert. The word started spreading that there was going to be a huge concert in Crab Alley Bay in two days.

Curtis and Oakley needed to get to West River. But how could they get there quickly? Now they only had one day left. It was starting to get dark so they found something to eat and then rested in the mud for the night.

The next morning it was raining. Curtis looked for Olivia to see if she would help. But he couldn't find her. Then Oakley found her on top of a sailboat and called to her.

"OLIVIA," yelled Oakley. Olivia heard him calling and flew over to see what he needed.

"How can I help you?" asked Olivia.

"Curtis and I need help getting to West River. Can you please help us?" asked Oakley.

"Sure, I know that old, red truck is going there for another party. I will drop you into the truck again," said Olivia.

It was raining so they didn't need to worry about drying up this time. They took a ride in the old, red truck, unnoticed by the men. When the truck finally stopped, men jumped out and slammed the truck doors and more men came running out of the restaurant. During all the commotion, Curtis and Oakley jumped off the truck and quickly jumped into the water.

They were in West River and had to find Bethany the Bass. She might be hard to find. She will be swimming and she may not even be near her home.

"How can we find Bethany? Curtis asked Oakley.

"If I remember correctly, bass love anchovies. So we just need to look for a school of anchovies and then we will find Bethany," said Oakley.

Curtis and Oakley searched the water for a school of anchovies but none were to be found. Then they saw something shining below them. They swam lower to see what it was. Could it be a school of anchovies to help them find Bethany? They swam closer.

It was a school of anchovies and a large bass was chasing the largest fish. Arthur the Anchovy swam quickly and hid in a crack

in the cave. Bethany lost her meal. She swam over to Curtis and Oakley.

"Hey guys, what's up?" asked Bethany.

"Sorry about scaring away your meal Bethany. Would you like to play the harp in a concert tomorrow? It's to help attract more crabs and oysters to the bay," said Curtis.

"Don't worry about the meal. There are plenty of fish in the bay. I would love to play the harp in the concert for you," said Bethany.

"Now we just need to find Sampson the Seahorse in Eastern Bay to play the flute, and Celia the Catfish in Crab Alley Bay to play the violin. Will you please help me find them?" asked Curtis.

"Sure, I will help you," said Bethany.

"Thanks for your help," said Curtis.

So Curtis, Oakley and Bethany needed a quick way to get to Eastern Bay to find Sampson the Seahorse. They looked for Olivia but she was nowhere around. Look! Bethany spotted a yellow sea plane in the water and they all jumped onto the plane.

The sea plane flew over the water and then over roads. It was so beautiful to see the water from the sky, but it was very scary. But they were all brave and they knew it was the only way to find Sampson.

Then Curtis noticed the old, red truck driving over the Chesapeake Bay Bridge. They all JUMPED off the plane and landed on the bed of the truck. Luckily Bethany landed in a bucket of melted ice.

Now they just needed a ride over the bridge to Eastern Bay to find Sampson. When the truck stopped, Curtis pushed the bucket of water over so Bethany could escape. But how would she get from the bed of the truck to the water? Could Olivia possibly be around? Yes, Oakley saw Olivia flying above them.

"OLIVIA!" yelled Oakley.

"How can I help you?" asked Olivia.

"Can you please gently pick up Bethany with your talons and place her into the water?" asked Oakley.

"You want me to pick up my favorite meal and let it go into the water?" asked Olivia.

"Yes, please, Olivia. There are plenty of fish in the bay. We need Bethany at the concert," said Oakley.

Olivia picked up the very scared Bethany and gently dropped her into the water. Then Olivia flew back to check on her family.

They were all getting tired and hungry again. They found something to eat and rested in the bottom of the bay for the night.

In the morning, they were off again. They needed to find Sampson the Seahorse. But how?

"We are running out of time. The concert is tonight and we still need to find Sampson the Seahorse and Celia the Catfish. Curtis, Oakley and Bethany swam towards the shore to look for Sampson. They found him hiding in the grasses.

"Sampson, would you like to play the flute in a concert tonight? It's to help attract more crabs and oysters to the bay," said Curtis.

"I would love to help," said Sampson.

"I need to find Celia the Catfish in Crab Alley Bay to play the violin. Will you please help me find her?" said Curtis.

"Sure, I will help you," said Sampson.

"Thanks for your help," said Curtis.

Curtis, Oakley, Bethany and Sampson were on their way to find Celia the Catfish in Crab Alley Bay. They agreed the quickest way to find Celia was to split up and then meet back in an hour. When they got back together, no one had been able to find her.

"Now what will we do? We need one more person who knows how to play the violin," said Curtis.

"Jordan the Jellyfish plays the violin. I played with her in another concert and she is very good," said Oakley.

"Jordan would be very good in the concert but she lives in Mayo Beach. We don't have time to go back that way to find her," said Curtis.

Just at that moment Jordan swam behind Curtis and said, "I heard you need a violin player. I can help you. When is the concert?"

They all yelled, "JORDAN!"

"We are so happy to see you Jordan. The concert is at 7:00 tonight. Can you make it?" asked Curtis.

"Sure, I would love to help you. I heard you were having the concert so that is why I am here. I wanted to see if I could help. Why are you having the concert tonight?" asked Jordan.

"We hope to attract more crabs and oysters to the bay. There aren't as many as there were years ago because of the toxins in the water from the factories and overfishing," said Curtis.

They started practicing for the concert in Crab Alley Bay and a crowd started gathering. There were anchovies, bass, catfish, crabs, crayfish, eels, flounder, gars, jellyfish, mussels, oysters, perch, rays, scallops, seahorses, sea stars, sharks and trout from all over the Chesapeake Bay.

When it was finally time to start the concert, there were so many crabs and oysters and other creatures of the bay that Curtis knew he did the right thing by having the concert and finding the perfect musicians.

Oakley the Oyster played the piano. Bethany the Bass played the harp. Sampson the Seahorse played the flute. Jordan the Jellyfish played the violin. Curtis the Crab played the cello.

They played some loud, high-energy songs and some soft, slow songs. All the songs were loved by the creatures of the bay. Some were even dancing.

Now they all could help spread the word to attract more crabs and oysters and clean up the Chesapeake Bay to make it a wonderful place for everyone.

Curtis the Crab and his friends ask YOU to help do your part too. Pick up your trash and put it in the trash cans or take it home with you. Don't harm or feed the animals at the parks. This will help keep the parks and beaches clean and help the creatures live long, healthy lives.

The End

FACTS ABOUT BLUE CRABS

1.   The blue crab is the most recognized creature in the Chesapeake Bay. They eat just about anything, including clams, oysters, mussels, smaller crustaceans, freshly dead fish, plant and animal debris and soft-shelled crabs.

2.   The blue crab's scientific name, Callinectes sapidus, comes from the Greek words for "beautiful" and "swimmer."

3.   Male blue crabs are known as "jimmies," while mature females are called "sooks."

4.   Crabs are found year-round in the Chesapeake Bay. Their range is from Nova Scotia to Argentina.

5.   In 1993, the harvest of blue crab was valued at around $100 million. Over the years, the crab population has decreased mainly due to water pollution and most of the soft-shelled crabs eaten are egg-producing females.

6.   In 2002, around two-thirds of the total United States market of blue crab came from four states – Louisiana (22%), North Carolina (17%), Maryland (14%), and Virginia (13%).

7.   The Chesapeake Bay, located in Maryland and Virginia, is famous for its blue crabs, and they are one of the most important economic items harvested from it.

8.   Hard-shelled blue crabs are steamed, and seasoned. The meat is picked and eaten from the body, legs and claws. Some of the delicacies prepared with crab meat are crab soup, crab cakes and crab dip.

9.   Natural predators of the blue crab are large fish like croakers and red drum; fish-eating birds like great blue herons; and sea turtles.

10.   Crabs can reach nine inches across. They have three pairs of walking legs, a pair of paddle-shaped swimming legs in the back and two large claws in the front of its body.

11.   The population of the blue crab has dramatically decreased in the Chesapeake Bay. The population fell from 900 million in 1993 to 300 million in 2008.

12.   Crabs are abundant in shallow water and bay grass beds during warm weather. They hibernate in the trenches of the Bay during the winter.

13.   Males spend more time in the fresher waters of the Bay and its rivers, while females congregate in saltier waters.

14.   The crabs start out with a greenish-blue color. When the pigment breaks down after cooking, the color changes to a bright orange.

15.   Each bright orange egg mass contains between 750,000 and two million eggs. The egg mass darkens as the developing larvae eat the orange yolk. In about two weeks, larvae are released into the salty waters near the mouth of the Bay.

16.   Currents transport blue crab larvae, called zoea, to the ocean, where they molt (lose their smaller shell) several times as they grow. Eventually, zoea return to the Bay and other estuaries.

17.   During their last larval molt, zoea change into a post-larval form called the megalops. Megalops crawl over the Bay's bottom to reach the upper Bay and its rivers.

18.   Megalops eventually change into immature crabs, which look like tiny adults. Immature crabs molt several times before they reach maturity, about 12 to 18 months after hatching.

19.   Blue crabs are bottom-dwelling crustaceans that use all of the Chesapeake Bay's habitats during the course of its life.

20.   Claws are bright blue. Mature females have red tips on their claws.

PLEASE HELP THE CHESAPEAKE BAY

The Chesapeake Bay is a gorgeous place to live, work and play. Check the website at www.cbf.org for more information on what you can do to help.

What can you do to help?
1. Become a member of the Chesapeake Bay Foundation and other Bay organizations.
2. Volunteer to help clean the Bay.
3. Join the Chesapeake Bay Action Network and speak out for the Bay!
4. Check the education section if you are a teacher. There are professional development initiatives, student education programs and more.
5. Throw trash in trash cans or take it with you.
6. Never throw anything into the Bay.
7. Never harm animals or dig up plants.
8. Help spread the word about the Bay.
9. Swim and fish in designated areas.

BOOKS WRITTEN
BY CINDY FRELAND

You will find books written by Cindy Freland on Amazon.com:

Pond Adventures with Aragon
Felix and the Purple Giant
Easy Guide to Your Facebook Business Page
Get a Job! Your Resume and Interview Guide
Monkey Farts: A Guide to Selling Your Handmade Crafts and Direct Sales Products
Easy and Free Self-Publishing: A Guide to Getting Your Book in Print and Kindle on Amazon
An American Virtual Assistant: The "Good, Bad and Ugly of Owning a Business Support Service
You Might Be Surprised: Marketing Ideas to Help Grow Your Business
Who Ate All The Apples? Lessons from my Brother
Mud Pies
No More Excuses: How to start a profitable business from your home on a shoestring budget
Jordan the Jellyfish: A Chesapeake Bay Adventure
Curtis the Crab: A Chesapeake Bay Adventure
Heather the Honey Bee: A Chesapeake Bay Adventure

Also place orders on our website at www.cbaykidsbooks.com.

Author:
Cindy Freland

Cindy Freland's inspiration comes from her love of children and animals. Most of her children's books are based on true events. She founded Maryland Secretarial Services, Inc. in 1997. She has won three business awards and teaches business workshops at two local community colleges, a senior center and two chamber of commerce offices. She offers word processing, data entry, desktop publishing and transcription to businesses of all sizes, government agencies, non-profit organizations and individuals throughout the United States. Her passion is teaching workshops, designing and managing Facebook pages and helping authors get their books on Amazon. She has written many business books, including one on Facebook for business, "Easy Guide to Your Facebook Business Page," and several children's books. You can find her books on www.amazon.com and books, t-shirts, and tote bags on www.cbaykidsbooks.com. Freland lives in Bowie, Maryland, with her family and dog, Juno.

Illustrator:
Jon Munson II

Jon C. Munson II is a digital artist and photographer. He also works with his parents supporting their lawn maintenance service, NaturaLawn of America. He enjoys spiritual pursuits, sailing, bowling, music, native instruments (Native American flute & drums), Legos, R/C trains, and many other interests. He lives in Bowie, Maryland, with his family. See examples of his art and photography below, and also by visiting http://jon-munson-ii.artistwebsites.com.

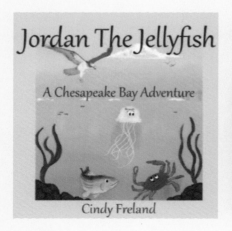

CPSIA information can be obtained
at www.ICGtesting.com
Printed in the USA
LVIC06n1731160517
534740LV00002B/17

9 781496 028006